Y0-DWM-551

To Abby's teacher,
Ms. Snider —
May good things
travel into your life!
Randi Lynn Mrvos

Saturn's Moon Press
(a division of Cactus Moon Publications)

Maggie and the Summer Vacation Show-and-Tell

For information please contact:
Cactus Moon Publications, LLC
1305 W. 7th Street, Tempe, AZ 85281
www.cactusmoonpublishing.com
ISBN: 978-0-9988932-7-3

First Edition

To Abby for bringing the love of picture books into my life
and Jim for being my biggest supporter.

It's the first day of school. I'm as happy as a dog with a bone...until Ms. Madison says, "Summer vacation show-and-tell."

She kicks off her fancy red shoes and tells us, "Bring something to share tomorrow!"

C
CAT
D
DOG
E
F

Everyone leaps from their seats with excitement except me. *I could say I hiked to the South Pole or...*

I could say I went on safari.

Maybe I could say I zoomed into space, to Mars, and to the Moon.

Freddie runs around the class like his pants are on fire.

"I'm going to bring a poison dart frog!" he yells.

Ms. Madison escorts him to his seat. She says, "As long as it stays in a cage."

At recess, I carry a box of chalk outside.

Emma draws a cactus. She says, "I'm bringing postcards from our trip out West."

Sara draws a seagull. She says, "I'm bringing seashells from the beach."

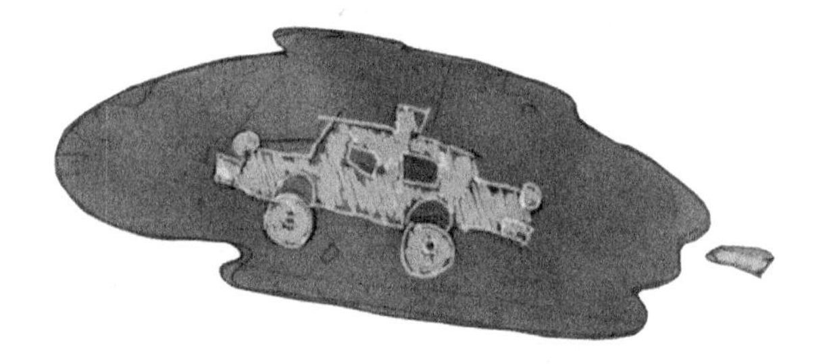

Ally draws a yellow car. "I went to New York City. I'm bringing a toy taxi."

Ally asks me, "What are you bringing, Maggie?"
I draw a big fat zero.

That night, over dinner Mom asks, “How was school?”

I tell her about show-and-tell and that I have nothing to share. “I wish we had gone on a trip.”

Mom asks, “Do you remember why we cancelled our plans?”

My dog, Trooper, jumps up and licks my face. “Yes, we found a hurt dog on the side of the road.”

William, my brother says, "I know, I know what you can bring. Remember when Grandma visited?"

He returns with a tray of teeth.

My family is not going to be much help.

After dinner, I take Trooper for a walk. As always, he sniffs everything. His favorite is trees. Tree trunks must smell like heaven.

When we get back home, I'm still thinking about show-and-tell. Snuggled up with Trooper, my eyes begin to fill with tears.

The next day in class Ms. Madison asks, “Who wants to go first?”

Freddie's arm shoots up.

"This is my poison dart frog!" shouts Freddie.

I wonder, *how did he keep that frog still while he painted it red?*

Sara shows her seashells.

Emma passes around postcards.

Ally lets everyone play with the taxi.

Now it's my turn. I carry a box to the front of the class. It's crammed with bandages, tape, scissors, and a white cotton sock.

"I didn't travel during my summer vacation, but this summer something special traveled into my life."

Mom peeks inside the classroom. When I nod, she lets go of the leash.

Trooper dashes into the classroom when he sees me. My friends hardly notice he has only three paws.

Trooper noses Emma's postcards and Ally's toy taxi while he checks out the room.

He stares down Freddie's frog.

He sneezes on Sara's seashell.

Trooper ends up at Ms. Madison's feet and sniffs her fancy red shoes.

Trooper comes to lick my face. He digs in the box I'm holding and chews the white cotton sock. I'm not surprised, he wore it for weeks.

I'm crazy about Trooper and he's crazy about me. I could talk about him forever.

MAGGIE AND THE SUMMER VACATION SHOW-AND-TELL

Discussion Guide

•What do you do on your summer vacation?

•Souvenirs are things that remind you of a vacation. What things remind you of your summer vacation? Do you have a favorite souvenir? What is it and where did it come from? What would you bring to school for Show and Tell if you didn't have a summer vacation souvenir?

•Maggie likes to compare things when she talks. She says she is as happy as a dog with a bone. What words can you use to finish the following sentences?

Maggie was as sad as a ________.
Trooper was as soft as a ________.
William was as silly as ________.

•Have you ever had a bad day at school? What happened that made it a bad day?

•Do you have a pet? Describe your pet. If you don't have a pet, what kind of pet would you like? Why?

•How does Maggie feel about Trooper? How can you tell?

•What kinds of things do pets need?

Introducing Charlie, the real inspiration behind Trooper

Charlie's Story

One chilly day in rural Kentucky, Kevin and Barbara Phillips and their children traveled on a country road to look for a farm for sale. As they drove past a pile of leaves, an animal lifted its head. Kevin and Barbara looked at each other and asked, "Was that a dog?"

Kevin stopped the van and found a skinny brown dog had made himself a bed of leaves by the side of the road. The dog was so weak that it couldn't raise its head again. It used his last bit of strength to get their attention. When Kevin got closer, the dog wagged its tail. Its back-left foot was missing. The dog was weak and sad-looking, but he had a beautiful face and eyes. The Phillips took him home with them and cared for him. In five days, he was able to stand again. He gradually got stronger and healthier. The Phillips called him Charlie and he became part of their family.

Charlie gives and receives affection genuinely and always has. He adores people and animals. He is kind and trusting. Most of all, he is loyal, of course, being a dog.

Charlie has been with the Phillips for ten years. Now, he is growing old and has gray whiskers. His favorite thing is to lie on the front porch while Kevin and Barbara sit outside. He loves to go on car rides and hang his head out the window with his ears flapping in the wind. When he goes on walks, he loves to make friends with everyone he meets. Charlie wants to be right next to Phillips all the time. He waits in a chair at the front window until they get home. He puts up with the other dog and two cats in the house, but knows he is the top dog.

Barbara says Charlie has taught her so much about unconditional love, trust, hope and never giving up. Charlie is her best friend.

Charlie

Saturn's Moon
Press

How the Moon Became Dim
by Ruth Wiseman
Illustrated by Clinton G. Bowers

Amazing
Alpha-Animals
Bob Harper

I Dream of
DRAGONS
Melissa Carrigee
Clinton G. Bowers

CPSIA information can be obtained
at www.ICGtesting.com
Printed in the USA
LVOW06*1033021017
550825LV00001B/2/P

9 780998 893273